The Emperor's
NIGHTINGALE
AND OTHER FEATHERY TALES

Written and Illustrated by

JANE RAY

BOXER BOOKS

With grateful thanks to Ann Jungman
for her expertise and help in researching these stories with me.
Jane Ray

First published in Great Britain in 2013
by Boxer Books Limited.
www.boxerbooks.com

The illustrations were prepared using Scraperboard, where the line is etched
onto a thin layer of white china clay on board coated with black India ink.

The text is set in Garamond.

ISBN 978-1-907152-59-7

1 3 5 7 9 10 8 6 4 2

Printed in China

All of our papers are sourced from managed forests and renewable resources.

In Memory of Kate Petty

CONTENTS

INTRODUCTION

People collect all sorts of things – stamps, cards or bus tickets, coins, shells or toy cars. Some people collect useful things like pieces of string and empty jam jars and buttons.

I collect stories.

I started as a child. I loved to hear my grandma telling me tales of when she was little. I devoured the serialised stories in the comics my sisters and I got every Saturday morning and waited impatiently for the following week's issue to find out what happened next. I loved being read to by my parents and my teachers.

I loved to tell stories too – the taller the better. I remember getting very upset that what I saw as a brilliant story, other people sometimes saw as a great big fib!

I retained all those stories, revisiting them in my head, imagining the characters and settings, sometimes rewriting the endings.

Now that I spend my days writing and illustrating books, I continue my collection. I'm always on the lookout for little scraps and snippets of stories. It may be something I've overheard on the bus, or part of a dream.

A phrase or description here, an intriguing beginning or a wonderful ending there, an amazing character or an extraordinary coincidence – all of these bits and pieces I file away in boxes in my mind. Every now and again I sift through them, stringing them together like beads on a necklace until suddenly they fall into place – beginning, middle and end.

And then there are the stories that belong to us all – the myths and legends and fairytales that are kept alive through constant retelling the world over. I love the fact that they have similar themes wherever they come from; people in Australia and France, Iraq and Ireland all seek love, happiness and good fortune, and fear death, sickness and war. Wherever we may come from, we are not so very different really.

Over the years I collected so many stories that I ran out of places to put them. In the end I decided to write them down in books, for you.

This first collection is full of stories about birds. As a child I used to climb up an apple tree in the garden, into the flickering green light of the leaves. If I sat still, really still, scarcely daring to breathe, a sparrow or a robin might fly into the tree and perch so close that I could look into its glittering eye and see its tiny heart beating under its feathers.

High up in the tree, I felt fleetingly a part of the bird world. I could watch people in the garden below, unobserved – a bird's eye view! I imagined taking off through the branches, feeling the freedom and exhilaration of soaring up into the sky.

Birds lift my spirits. They bring me happiness and evoke a sense of the seasons. A blackbird's song is springtime; a pigeon's soft, throaty call is summer; the raucous cry of crows means autumn and bare winter branches; and the robin is midwinter, a splash of russet against the snow.

Of course, I am not alone – birds have always fascinated humankind. They have delighted artists, poets and musicians since time began and inspired many wonderful stories. It is these stories that I have collected here to share with you. They have flown from places far and near, winging their way from Africa and India, Russia, China and Germany. Some are about real birds, from the little swallow to the stately heron; others feature birds from our imaginations, the mythological and fantastic. Some of the stories in this collection I have known all my life – fairytales nested so deep in my heart that I can't remember when I first heard them. Others were new to me, told by friends or discovered in libraries. Many are folktales or myths, the sorts of stories that are handed on from generation to generation, owned by everybody and nobody, and subtly shaped by each retelling.

I hope these stories sing for you as they do for me – and carry you away on bright wings.

THE HAPPY PRINCE

I love to see the first swallows of summer swooping across a blue sky and then later, lining up on telephone wires before flying south for the winter. This story was originally written by Oscar Wilde in 1888, one of his intensely moving fairy tales. It is a rare example of a story that doesn't have a happy ending, yet is somehow uplifting. I have changed some aspects of the story that are rather old-fashioned to our 21st century ears, but in essence it is still the story that I have always loved about a statue and a kind-hearted little swallow.

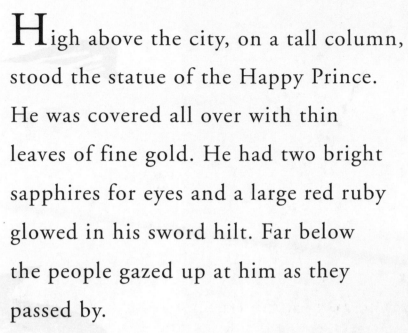

High above the city, on a tall column, stood the statue of the Happy Prince. He was covered all over with thin leaves of fine gold. He had two bright sapphires for eyes and a large red ruby glowed in his sword hilt. Far below the people gazed up at him as they passed by.

"How handsome our Happy Prince looks," said the doctor, out on his rounds.

"Look at the way he shines in the sun!" said the children as they hurried to school.

"We are very fortunate to have such a wonderful statue to grace our city," said the

mayor. "It is so important to impress the
visitors who come here."

One autumn day, a flock of swallows
swooped low across the city rooftops.
"Where are they all going?" asked a

little boy who was walking
home with his mother.
"They are all flying
south for the winter,"
she said.
"It is far too cold for
them here and they'd die
if they stayed. But don't
worry, they'll be back in the spring!"

But one little swallow left the flock
and came to rest on the golden head
of the Happy Prince. This bird had a

soul and was entranced by the golden
autumn leaves as they fluttered and spun
to the ground.

"Aren't you coming with us?" asked
the other swallows as they looped once
more around the statue. "It will be very
cold soon."

"Of course I'm coming," said the
little swallow, "just not quite yet. I'll
stay another day or two, until the leaves
have fallen. Then I will join you in the
sun in Egypt!"

"Don't leave it too long!"
called the rest of the flock, and
off they flew,
southward
to the sun.

The swallow sat for a while and then swooped down into the square below and picked up some crumbs from outside the baker's shop. When his stomach was full he felt ready for sleep and he decided to rest at the feet of the Happy Prince.

"I have a golden bedroom," he said softly to himself as he looked around. But just as he was putting his head under his wing a large drop of water fell on him.

'Oh, bother, it must be raining,' thought the swallow. He looked up and – plop! – another drop fell. "Oh, what is the use of a statue if it cannot keep the rain off?" he said. "I shall go and find a good chimney pot to sleep in."

The swallow opened his wings and prepared to take off. But just at that moment another drop fell. He looked up and saw that the eyes of the Happy Prince were filled with tears. Large, wet drops rolled down his golden cheeks. His face was so beautiful in the moonlight that the little swallow was filled with pity.

"Whatever is the matter?" he said, as he flew up to the prince's shoulder.

"When I was alive," said the statue, "I lived a life of luxury in a magnificent palace where sorrow was not allowed to enter. I wore beautiful clothes, ate delicious food and slept in fine linen sheets. A great wall ran around the palace gardens and I never bothered to ask what lay beyond it. I was the most contented man in the whole world. Everyone called me the Happy Prince."

"How very nice," said the swallow.

"But then I died," continued the statue, "and because I was so young and so loved, they built this beautiful statue of me and set it high above the rooftops."

The little swallow still couldn't see why the statue was crying. "So now you have the best view in all the city!" he said. "What can possibly be the problem?"

"Don't you see?" said the statue. "From here I can see all the misery and unhappiness that was hidden from me when I was alive. Even though my heart is made of lead, the suffering I see makes me weep. Do you see that tiny attic window, way over there, with the flickering candle?"

"What about it?" asked the swallow.

"I can see a poor woman seated there. She has been working all night, embroidering a ball gown for a rich lady.

Her eyes are tired and her little boy is
ill in bed. He cries for oranges, but the
woman is so poor she cannot buy them.
Swallow, little swallow, take her the ruby

from my sword hilt."

"I need my sleep before
I start the long journey to
Egypt," said the swallow.
"But I daresay I can
manage to do that for you,"
he added, for he had
a kind heart.

So the swallow took the ruby from
the sword hilt and flew with it across the
city, past the cathedral tower and over
the river until he reached the woman's
windowsill. He saw that she had fallen

asleep over her work, so he flew in and
dropped the ruby onto the silk gown.
Then he flew around the little boy,
gently fanning his forehead and cooling
his fever.

"It's odd," the swallow said to the
prince on his return, "I feel warm, even
though it is getting so cold." Then he
tucked his head under his wing and
went to sleep.

The next morning the little swallow
flew to the river and watched the last of
the red and gold leaves float down into
the water. He stayed there all day, and as
the moon rose he returned to the statue
of the Happy Prince.

"I must leave now," he said. "It is

getting chilly and I'm going to Egypt."

"Dear little swallow," said the prince,
"you did a wonderful thing last night.
But now I can see a young man,
a writer, who lives in a shabby garret.
He is trying to finish a great book full
of wonderful thoughts and ideas, but
he has no money for food. He is cold
and hungry."

"Oh, very well," said the swallow,
who really had a very good heart. "Shall
I take him another ruby?"

"I'm afraid I have only the sapphires
of my eyes left now. Pluck one out and
take it to him."

"Don't ask me to do such a dreadful
thing, dear prince," said the swallow.

"How will you manage without your eye?"

"How will the writer manage without food?" said the prince.
"Please, do as I ask you."

So the swallow plucked out the prince's eye and flew with the sapphire across the city and in through a hole in the writer's roof.

As he flew back to the statue he noticed how very cold it was becoming.

"Now I really must leave for Egypt. I can delay no longer," the swallow informed the prince.

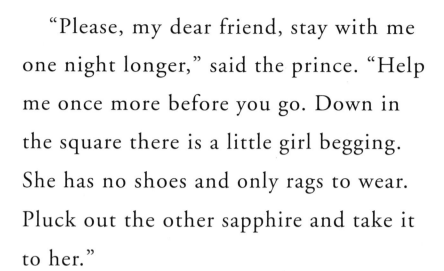

"Please, my dear friend, stay with me one night longer," said the prince. "Help me once more before you go. Down in the square there is a little girl begging. She has no shoes and only rags to wear. Pluck out the other sapphire and take it to her."

The swallow began to weep. "Dear prince," he said, "how can you ask me to do such a thing? I cannot pluck out your other eye. How will you see?"

"Swallow, little swallow," said the prince, "the child is living and I am not – do as I command you."

So the swallow took the other sapphire to the child in the street and returned to the prince.

"You are blind now," he said, "so I will stay with you."

"No, little swallow," said the prince, "you must go to Egypt."

"I will stay with you always," said the swallow, and he curled up and went to sleep at the prince's feet.

The next day the swallow flew over the great city and saw the rich making merry while the poor starved in the streets. He saw children who were hungry, frightened and cold. He flew back to the prince's shoulder and told him all he had seen.

"I am covered with fine gold," said the prince. "Take it off, leaf by leaf, and give it to the poor."

Leaf after leaf of gold the swallow picked off, until the Happy Prince looked quite dull and grey. Leaf after leaf he brought to the poor, and the children's faces grew rosy and they began to laugh again.

Then the snow came, and after the snow came the frost. The poor little swallow grew colder and colder, but he would not leave the prince. He tried to keep warm by flapping his wings, but at last he knew he was going to die. He summoned all his strength and flew up to the prince's shoulder one last time.

"Goodbye, dear prince," he whispered.

"I'm glad you are going to Egypt at last, my friend," said the prince. "Kiss me before you go, for I love you."

The swallow fluttered at the prince's lips, kissed him and then fell dead at his feet. At that moment there was a strange crack from inside the statue, as if something had broken. The prince's lead heart had snapped right in two. It certainly was a very hard frost.

The people of the city had begun to notice how shabby the statue had become.

"Whatever has happened to our Happy Prince?" demanded the mayor.

"His gold is all gone, and his jewels. He is little better than a beggar. What will people think?" He gave orders for the statue to be pulled down and for a new one of himself to be put in its place.

The statue was melted down in a great furnace but, strangely, the broken lead heart would not melt. It was thrown on a rubbish heap, where the body of the swallow also lay.

An angel flew over the city. Below her she could see the glittering steeples and golden spires. She saw the great palace, and the river and the glorious merchant ships with their billowing sails. But as she flew over the rubbish heap she saw the broken lead heart and the dead

swallow. '*I shall take these broken things to God,*' she thought, 'for they are the most precious things in this whole city.'

MULUNGU PAINTS THE BIRDS

A friend told me this story, an African myth from Kenya. Mulungu is a supreme creator god of the Nyamwezi people of Tanzania in eastern Africa. I just loved the idea of Mulungu, the hugely powerful Creator of All Things, sitting down on a little wooden stool and patiently painting each bird with his little painting stick.

When the world began, all the birds were alike. They were different shapes and sizes, of course – some had long necks or spindly legs, and others had elaborate tail feathers or curly crests on their heads. But none of them had any marks or patterns or splashes of colour – they were all just white, all the same.

When the birds looked around them they saw beautiful flowers of scarlet and pink blowing in the wind. They saw the butterflies, with their blue and yellow wings, dancing in the sunlight. They looked at each other and they felt themselves to be very dull indeed.

One day the parrot gathered the other birds around her and said, "Let's pray to the Great Creator Mulungu and ask if he can make us all different colours. I, for one, have always fancied a scarlet tail. Next time he's got his paint pots out, I'm sure it would be no trouble!"

"What a splendid idea!" said the weaverbird. "I've always longed to be yellow and black!"

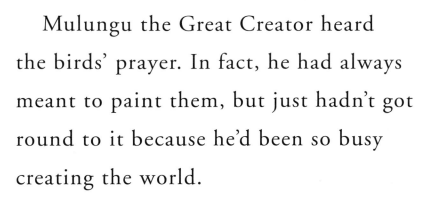

Mulungu the Great Creator heard
the birds' prayer. In fact, he had always
meant to paint them, but just hadn't got
round to it because he'd been so busy
creating the world.

So, when he had some time, he sat
down on his stool with his paint pots
at his feet and gathered all the birds
together in rows.

Mulungu called each in turn, letting
them hop onto his finger, or sitting
them gently on his knee. He took up his
little painting stick, carefully chose his
colours and decorated each bird before
letting them go to dry their feathers in
the sun.

He painted the sunbird in vibrant

green, purple, red and blue. He gave the
lovebird a sweet peach-coloured face and
the hoopoe handsome black and white
stripes and a russet-coloured crest.

Now, the boubou is a fussy bird
who is forever running up and down,
cheeping and twittering, trying to
attract attention at all costs. He was
near the end of the row but he couldn't

wait for his turn. He was very impatient, behaving like a spoilt child, hopping up and down saying, "Me next! Me next!"

At first Mulungu ignored him, determined to make him wait for his turn. He painted the cuckoo emerald green and the little kingfisher purple and blue. But still the boubou kept clamouring and fussing. Mulungu was

in the middle of painting the legs of the
common stilt red when he put down his
stick and beckoned the boubou forward.
"All right," he said, "have it your way.
I'll paint you next."

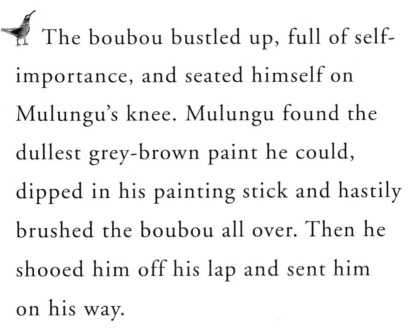 The boubou bustled up, full of self-importance, and seated himself on Mulungu's knee. Mulungu found the dullest grey-brown paint he could, dipped in his painting stick and hastily brushed the boubou all over. Then he shooed him off his lap and sent him on his way.

And that is why, even to this day, the boubou is the only bird with such drab grey feathers among the glorious rose-ringed parakeets and red-billed finches, the yellow wagtails and golden pipits and all the other brilliantly plumed birds who glitter like jewels in the African bush.

THE OWL
AND THE PUSSYCAT

This is one of those poems that everybody knows and can't quite remember where they first heard it. Edward Lear was a master of the absurd and the nonsensical – does anyone know what a 'runcible spoon' is? Or the 'Bong-tree'? Only you can supply the answers!

The Owl and the Pussycat
went to sea
In a beautiful pea-green boat,
They took some honey,
and plenty of money,
Wrapped up in a
five-pound note.
The Owl looked up
to the stars above,
And sang to a small guitar,
"O lovely Pussy!
O Pussy my love,
What a beautiful Pussy you are,
You are,
You are!
What a beautiful Pussy you are!"

Pussy said to the Owl,

"you elegant fowl!

How charmingly sweet you sing!

O let us be married!

Too long we have tarried:

But what shall we do for a ring?"

They sailed away,

for a year and a day,

To the land where

the Bong-tree grows

And there in a wood

a Piggy-wig stood

With a ring at the end of his nose,

His nose,

His nose,

With a ring at the end of his nose.

"Dear Pig,
are you willing
to sell for one shilling
your ring?"
Said the Piggy,
"I will."

So they took it away,
and were married next day
By the Turkey
who lives on the hill.
They dined on mince,
and slices of quince,
Which they ate with
a runcible spoon;

And hand in hand,

on the edge

of the sand,

They danced by the light

of the moon,

The moon,

The moon,

They danced by the light of the moon.

NOAH'S ARK

Mankind has always lived in fear of the Apocalypse — some dreadful, unstoppable disaster that ends life on Earth as we know it. There are many different versions of the flood story told by cultures all over the world. Today, the image of the dove with an olive branch in her beak is an internationally recognised symbol of peace and hope.

One day God gazed down on the Earth and despaired. Everywhere he looked he saw people fighting and hurting each other. He saw greed and selfishness, cruelty and waste. Sadly he decided to wipe the Earth clean and start again.

But having thought about it for a while, he changed his mind. He looked at the beautiful creatures below him — the great elephants and the feathered birds, the leaping gazelles and scurrying mice, and he couldn't bear to destroy them all. And there was one man called

Noah, who was a good, kind, hard-working man.

So God thought hard until he came up with a plan. Then he called down to Noah, "I am going to make it rain for forty days and forty nights. There will be such a great flood that everything on

Earth will die. But I am placing all my trust in you."

You can imagine how afraid Noah must have felt, but he had great faith in God. He said, "I'm listening – tell me what you want me to do." So God told Noah his plan.

"You must make an ark, a huge boat, of gopher wood. It will have lots of rooms and will be covered inside and out with pitch to make it watertight. It shall be three hundred cubits long, fifty cubits wide and thirty cubits high. It will have windows, and a door in the side, and it will be three storeys high." Noah wrote this all down and tried not to panic.

God went on: "When the ark is finished, you must move in, with your wife and your sons, Shem, Ham and Japheth, and their three wives too." Noah was relieved – at least his family would be saved.

But then God continued: "Now, I want you to bring two of every living thing into the ark, male and female – birds of the air, and beasts of the fields and mountains and woodlands. Don't forget anything – two of everything, even the tiny creeping creatures, worms and ants and

earwigs and slugs – yes, even slugs. And you must take in all the food that the animals eat, and food for you too of course."

Noah was quite overwhelmed by what God was asking him to do, but he was determined to do it.

When, after seven days, the heavens opened and it began to rain, Noah and his family were ready. Every storey of the ark was filled with snorting, roaring, stamping, howling animals. The storerooms were packed with food – grains and roots, fruit, vegetables, nuts and hay. There were pickles and jams, dried fish, salted hams and cheeses.

The rain fell steadily. It poured, it streamed and it rushed. Everything was drowned – even the highest houses and the tallest trees were covered. The valleys became rivers and still the waters rose, until even the hills and the mountains had disappeared.

The ark looked tiny on the endless
stretch of grey water, under a lowering sky.
Inside the ark it was dark and cramped
and smelly with all those animals.

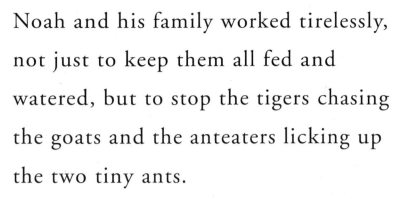

Noah and his family worked tirelessly, not just to keep them all fed and watered, but to stop the tigers chasing the goats and the anteaters licking up the two tiny ants.

The forty days and nights of endless rain were long and difficult and it was hard for Noah and his family to keep their spirits up. But God didn't forget them. At last, when the time was right, he made a soft wind blow over the water and the rain gradually eased and then stopped. The water began to subside and the ark came to rest on the great mountains of Ararat.

One morning Noah opened a window
and released a raven into the bright sky.
A few hours later the bird returned,
exhausted because the waters were still
well above the treetops and she had
found nowhere to perch. Some days
later Noah released a dove, and this time
the bird returned with an olive branch
in her beak. Noah knew that the waters
were draining away from the Earth at
last. After seven more days, Noah sent
the dove out again. This time she didn't
return, and Noah knew that she had
found somewhere safe to start building
a nest.

There was great excitement on the
ark. The doors were flung open and
sunshine streamed in. All around, the

Earth was dry and life was returning.
Noah looked up at the open sky with
relief and gratitude in his heart. Above
him was a great bow of colours arching
across the pale blue sky.

God spoke to Noah again: "I have
set my bow, my rainbow, in the sky.
It is my promise to you and to every
living creature that I will never destroy
the Earth again. You can go now, out
of the ark – all the animals and birds
and insects – and replenish the Earth.
I promise you that all will be well.
From this day on, seedtime and harvest,
winter's cold and summer's heat, the
light of day and the starry night will
never cease."

HOPE IS THE THING WITH FEATHERS

Hope is the thing with feathers

That perches in the soul,

And sings the tune without

the words,

And never stops at all,

And sweetest in the gale is heard;

And sore must be the storm

That could abash the little bird

That kept so many warm.

I've heard it in the chillest land,

And on the strangest sea;

Yet, never, in extremity,

It asked a crumb of me.

– Emily Dickinson

THE GOLDEN SWAN

Swans are the most regal and serene of birds, and the idea of a swan with feathers of gold is irresistible. This story from India has the same moral as the rather better-known fable by Aesop, The Goose that Laid the Golden Egg, and is a stern warning against greed.

There was once a woman who lived in a little tumbledown house with her two young daughters. They were very poor – they often went hungry and their clothes were patched and torn.

Not far from the tumbledown house was a pond, and on the pond lived a beautiful swan with feathers of the purest gold. As she swam serenely through the water, the swan couldn't help but notice just how poor the family were and how hard they had to struggle to live. They were all dressed in rags and ate nothing but dry bread and dahl. The swan had a kind heart and thought to herself, 'If I gave them one of my golden feathers, they could sell it and buy good food.'

So she flew into the house where the woman was sitting, huddled and miserable, with her two

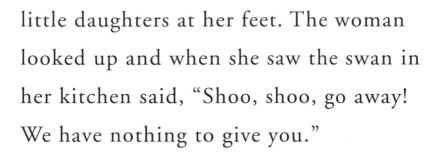

little daughters at her feet. The woman looked up and when she saw the swan in her kitchen said, "Shoo, shoo, go away! We have nothing to give you."

But the swan plucked one of her precious feathers and laid it in the woman's lap before flying away with a great flapping of her golden wings.

The woman couldn't believe her eyes. She laughed and shouted with joy, "I can sell this golden feather at the market and buy food – bread and meat and fruit!" The little girls clapped their hands and danced around the kitchen.

A few days later the swan visited the woman and her daughters again. They looked well fed now and there was plenty of food in the cupboard. But the swan plucked another feather from her wing and left it at the woman's feet.

The woman was delighted. "I can sell this feather at the market and buy new clothes and shoes for us to wear!" she cried. And the little girls laughed and skipped around the garden!

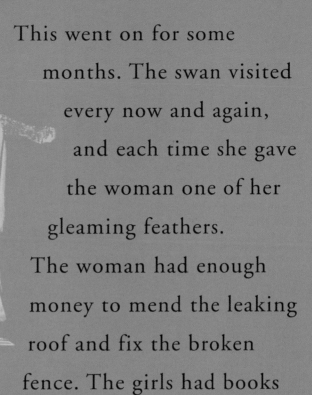

This went on for some
months. The swan visited
every now and again,
and each time she gave
the woman one of her
gleaming feathers.
The woman had enough
money to mend the leaking
roof and fix the broken
fence. The girls had books
and toys, new saris and pretty slippers
on their little feet. They began to relax
and enjoy living in comfort.

But one day,
the woman realised
that the swan hadn't
visited for a while.

"What will we do if the
swan stops coming?" she
said to her daughters.
"I need silk shawls and
bright carpets and bangles
of gold. I want silver anklets
with little bells on, and I saw such
soft woollen blankets in the market
last week … Next time the swan visits
I think we should grab her and pluck
all her feathers. Then we'll never be
poor again!"

The little girls looked at each
other in horror. "But you can't do
that, Mama!" said one. "You will
hurt the swan, and she is our friend."

But the woman could think of

nothing but all the new things she wanted – copper pots and pans to replace the old tin ones she cooked with, silk at the windows instead of cotton, flowers in the garden instead of vegetables.

So the next time the swan glided down into the garden, the woman grabbed her and began to pull out all the poor creature's feathers. But as she plucked them, they changed from shimmering golden plumes to ordinary

chicken feathers, fluttering and blowing all over the garden.

The swan wrenched herself free of the greedy woman's grasp and, with a great sad cry, she flew away and never, ever came back.

JORINDA AND JORINGEL

I love the dark atmosphere of this story. I can imagine the forest, a place of beauty but also of fear, and the poor trapped birds, fluttering in their cages and longing for freedom. It was written by the Grimm brothers but is not as well known as many of their other stories.

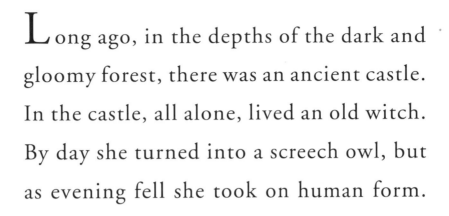

Long ago, in the depths of the dark and gloomy forest, there was an ancient castle. In the castle, all alone, lived an old witch. By day she turned into a screech owl, but as evening fell she took on human form.

The old witch had the power to lure any wild beast or bird to her cooking pot, and she lived well.

If any young man came within a hundred paces of the crumbling castle walls, he would be rooted to the spot as if turned to stone, unable to move until the old witch chose to release him. And if a young girl came near the castle, she would be transformed into a bird. Then the witch would catch her and put her in a cage that she would hang in the castle. Seven thousand cages hung there, each one containing a beautiful bird – larks and robins, wrens and finches – feathers gleaming, but heads bowed in despair and sorrow.

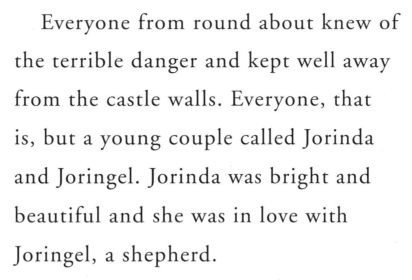

Everyone from round about knew of the terrible danger and kept well away from the castle walls. Everyone, that is, but a young couple called Jorinda and Joringel. Jorinda was bright and beautiful and she was in love with Joringel, a shepherd.

One summer evening they were walking together through the forest. It was wonderful to be among the trees; the sunbeams slanted between the trunks, and the turtle doves called mournfully in the dappled shade. Jorinda and Joringel were so in love, staring into each other's eyes as they walked, that they scarcely even noticed the beauty around them. They wandered

from the path they knew and when they
looked up they realised they were lost.

Suddenly they came upon the
looming grey walls of the castle. Joringel
grabbed Jorinda by the hand. "Quick,
we must run!" But he realised with
horror that he held not Jorinda's soft
hand but a feather. Jorinda had become
a tiny feathered bird, a linnet, fluttering
in panic before his eyes. He tried to
hold her in his cupped hands, crying,
"Oh, Jorinda, my sweet girl! Come back
to me!" But his limbs were like stone
and his voice was silenced.

A screech owl with eyes like glowing
coals flew around them – once, twice,
three times – calling, "To-woo, to-woo,

to-woo." Then it disappeared into the darkening trees.

The last rays of the sun vanished and a shadowy chill descended on the forest. Then out of the trees came the ancient witch, dressed in rags and tatters.

"Another pretty one for my collection!" she cackled. She reached out and snatched up the linnet in her claw-like hand and scurried back into the forbidding castle.

Try as he might, Joringel could not move. Later, much later, when the moon had risen, the witch returned. She crept around him, muttering strange spells. Gradually Joringel's limbs began to loosen, until at last he was free to move. He fell on his knees before the old woman. "Please release my beautiful Jorinda," he cried. "Take me instead!"

"Never!" cackled the witch. "You will never see your sweetheart again!" And she hobbled off into the castle.

Joringel was heartbroken. He wept and lamented, "What shall I do?"

could not bear to return to his village where everyone knew him and his beloved Jorinda. Instead he walked until he came to another village and there he settled, tending sheep. Whenever he could he walked back to the old castle, not too near of course, hoping to catch a glimpse of Jorinda's soft feathers.

The weeks went on and turned to months. One night Joringel's troubled sleep was broken by a dream. In his dream he found an extraordinary flower of deep crimson red with a pearl in its centre. He picked the flower and went with it into the castle. Everything he touched with this flower was freed from enchantment, including Jorinda.

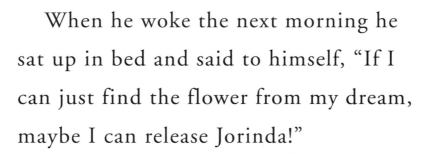
When he woke the next morning he sat up in bed and said to himself, "If I can just find the flower from my dream, maybe I can release Jorinda!"

He leapt out of bed and set off across the hills, determined to find the magical bloom. For eight days he searched high and low but found nothing. Then on the ninth day, just as the sun was rising, he saw it – a beautiful crimson flower with a dewdrop in its centre like the finest pearl.

He travelled back through night and day until he was within one hundred paces of the castle. He drew closer, but with the flower in his hand he was not

turned to stone. He strode boldly up to the castle door and flung it open.

"Jorinda!" he called. "It's me, Joringel. I'm here to rescue you!"

He walked into the castle courtyard. In the distance, he could hear the faint sound of birds singing. He followed the sad song until he came to a huge marble hall. There was the witch, feeding the birds in the seven thousand cages. At the sound of his footsteps she turned and screamed, "Out! Out! Get out of my castle or I'll turn you to stone!" But the flower protected Joringel from harm, and the witch, spitting and snarling with fury, was powerless to hurt him.

But how was Joringel to find
Jorinda? So many cages, so many birds,
all singing with new hope and fluttering
at the bars of their prisons.

Then, from the corner of his eye, he saw the witch quietly pick up a cage and creep towards the door. Swiftly he snatched the cage from her hands and touched both her and the cage with the magical flower.

Now, no matter how she shrieked and spat, the witch no longer had the power to bewitch or enchant. And there before him stood Jorinda, freed of her feathers and as beautiful as ever.

"Oh, my dearest Joringel," she cried. "I knew you would come!"

Quickly they ran around all the cages, touching each with the crimson flower, opening the doors and turning all the birds back into young girls again.

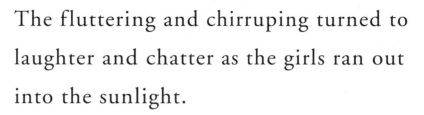

The fluttering and chirruping turned to laughter and chatter as the girls ran out into the sunlight.

Then Jorinda and Joringel, hand in hand, wandered home through the forest and, of course, they lived happily ever after.

HERON AND HUMMINGBIRD

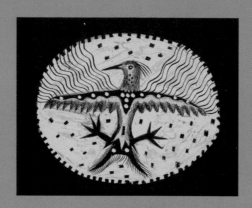

I love this Native American Indian story. There is a real sense of the particular characteristics of the heron and the hummingbird, which must have come about through the close observation and love of the birds by the Hitchiti people. The moral is the same as Aesop's Tortoise and Hare story.

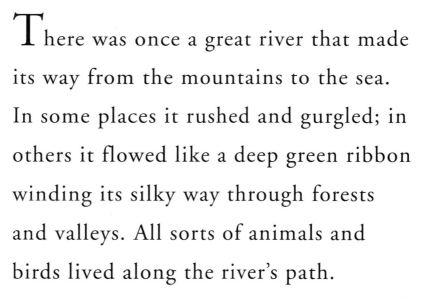

There was once a great river that made its way from the mountains to the sea. In some places it rushed and gurgled; in others it flowed like a deep green ribbon winding its silky way through forests and valleys. All sorts of animals and birds lived along the river's path.

Heron and Hummingbird were good friends even though they were very different, both in looks and in character. Hummingbird was a tiny bundle of colour, full of fun. He spent his days flitting from place to place, catching a little silver fish here, sipping sweet nectar from a flower there, chasing sunbeams and bumblebees.

Heron was bigger and slower and quieter. She sat for hours at a time, deep in thought, occasionally swooping down to scoop a fish from the river in her great bill.

One long, hot summer when there had been no rain for weeks and weeks, the river began to dry up. The muddy banks were cracked and dry and the fish became fewer and fewer. Hummingbird said to Heron, "I'm not sure there are enough fish in the river for both of us. We must have a race to decide who is going to own the fish that are left."

Heron thought for a moment and said, "We'll race to the tall tree just before the waterfall. It will take all day."

They agreed to start at dawn the following morning. Whoever was sitting at the top of the tree by sunset would own all the fish in the river.

Hummingbird said to himself, "I'm sure I will win. I may be small but I'm fast, and I can zip and flit around as quick as quick. I'm going to enjoy this!"

As the sun rose next morning, the two birds perched on a rock in the middle of the river. News of their race had got around and all the other animals and birds were out to cheer them on and shout encouragement.

Heron stretched her great wings in
the sun and thought about the journey
ahead. Hummingbird was impatient
to set off and, as the first beam of the
rising sun lit the water, both birds rose
into the air.

Heron flapped steadily and patiently,
her long legs trailing behind and her
neck craned forward. Hummingbird

zipped past her singing, "You'll have to go faster than that, my friend. Look at the speed I'm doing!"

And indeed Hummingbird had got off to a fine start. He sped along, a bright ball of green and blue feathers, iridescent in the morning sunshine.

As the sun rose higher in the sky, Hummingbird, well ahead, looked over his shoulder and sniggered, "Look at old Heron flapping like a broken 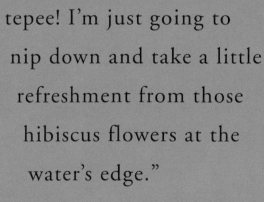 tepee! I'm just going to nip down and take a little refreshment from those hibiscus flowers at the water's edge."

Down he sped,

hovering in front of
the beautiful flowers and
drinking deep from their delicious
nectar. Heron flew on, following the
wide green band of the river and feeling
the heat of the sun on her back. After a
while she saw a flash of green and blue
flitting in and out of the flowers on the
bank far below. She smiled to herself
as she overtook Hummingbird and
continued her stately progress.

Hummingbird, realising that Heron
was now in the lead, quickly flew ahead
and overtook her on the bend of the
river. But not long after that he met
some butterflies and, since Heron was
again so far behind, he stayed awhile to

dance and play.

And so they continued all day long –
first Hummingbird took the lead, before
being distracted by pretty flowers full of
nectar or friends calling up to him, then
Heron overtook him and eventually
Hummingbird caught up. The shadows
grew longer and Hummingbird began to
feel tired. He glanced over his shoulder.
"No sign of poor old Heron. She's doing
her best but I don't think I need worry,"
he said to himself. He stopped to rest
in a willow tree. He was so full of sweet
nectar that he grew sleepy and before
long he dozed off, his tiny green head
drooping to his breast. As dusk began
to fall Heron flapped past him,

the long, even strokes of her great wings pulling her on and on.

The sun began to sink behind the mountain and a little breeze sprang up and ruffled Hummingbird's feathers. He stretched and opened one eye. 'Oh well,' he thought, 'I suppose I'd better go and win this race.' He sprang into the air, refreshed and full of life, and zip-zipped around the last curve in the river towards the tall tree. Imagine his surprise as he rounded the bend and saw Heron sitting sleek and calm at the very top of the tree!

"Well, good evening, my friend," she said. "What kept you?"

Ever since
that day, Heron
has owned all
the fish in the
river, big and
small. And
Hummingbird —
he drinks only
the nectar from
the flowers on
the bank.

THE EMPEROR'S NIGHTINGALE

This well-known story by Hans Christian Andersen has always delighted me. The contrast between the ornate pomposity of court life and the simplicity and freedom of the nightingale is appealing. I love the character of the nightingale — she is full of common sense, as well as compassion. There is a purity to her character that is reflected in her ability to sing so beautifully.

Long ago the Emperor of China lived
in an exquisite palace made of the finest
porcelain. The palace was surrounded by
a beautiful garden that bloomed in every
season. There were lakes and fountains,
and flowers of every colour. Beyond
the garden was a wood with trees that
reached out over a deep blue lake.

In the wood lived a little nightingale who sang so sweetly that even the busy fisherman paused to listen to her as he cast his nets. "How beautiful!" he said, before getting back to work.

The Emperor's palace was famous the world over. People came from far and wide to marvel at its beauty. Many of

them were so inspired that they wrote books and songs and poems about the wonders they had seen there. But if they heard the song of the nightingale, they always said, "This is the most wonderful thing of all!"

The Emperor loved to read

everything that was written in praise of his palace and gardens. But since he had never ventured into the woods, he had never heard the nightingale.

"The nightingale?" he said. "What is this about? Why have I never heard it?"

"Indeed, Sire," said the chamberlain, "I have never heard it either. It has most certainly never been presented at court."

"I demand that the nightingale be brought to sing to me this very evening," roared the Emperor, "or heads will roll!"

But where was the nightingale to be found? No one seemed to know and, as the day went on, the inhabitants of the palace became more and more nervous. At last, a young kitchen maid came forward.

"Oh yes, sirs, I can take you to the nightingale. I know her very well. I pass her on my way home and I often stop to listen to her song."

They set off for the wood, the little kitchen maid leading the way and

half the court, in their fine shoes and
flowing silken robes, following behind.

As they struggled through the mud
and brambles, a sound rang out.

"Ah!" sighed a courtier. "That must be
the nightingale! What a glorious sound!"
The kitchen maid giggled. "Oh no, sir,
that is not the nightingale. That is a cow!

We still have a long way to go."

Deeper into the wood they went, and soon another sound was heard ringing through the trees.

"Stop!" cried the chamberlain. "I think I hear it! Exquisite!"

Again the kitchen maid laughed. "How is it that all you clever people don't know the croaking of a frog from the song of a nightingale?"

Just at that moment, the nightingale began to sing.

"There it is!" said the girl. "Listen – oh, listen! She is sitting up there." And she pointed to a small grey bird high up in the branches.

"Such a drab little bird," murmured
the courtiers, "but, oh, what a beautiful
song!" And they stood transfixed
listening to her sing.

"Little nightingale," called the
kitchen maid gently, "our gracious
Emperor wants you to sing for him."

"I would be delighted!" said the nightingale, and she sang a song so beautiful that it was a joy to hear.

"Did the Emperor enjoy that?" she asked when she had finished.

"Goodness, the Emperor is not here," said the chamberlain. "You must come with us to the palace and sing for him there."

"I will come if you wish it," said the nightingale, "though my song sounds sweeter in the open air."

"The Emperor cannot possibly walk through the mud and the brambles like any common person," replied the chamberlain. "You must come with us to the palace."

So the nightingale followed them all
back to the palace. In the great hall,
the Emperor and the rest of the court
gathered around a golden cage
with a golden perch.

"Welcome, little
nightingale," said the
Emperor, and nodded his
head for her to begin.

The nightingale opened
her beak and her sweet
song flowed around the
great echoing hall. She sang so sweetly
that tears filled the Emperor's eyes and
ran down his cheeks. When she saw
this, the nightingale sang
even more sweetly and her song

went straight to his heart.

The Emperor was so delighted that he proclaimed that the nightingale should stay at court and sing for him whenever he commanded. She was to live in the golden cage and be allowed out twice a day in the company of twelve servants, each holding a silken ribbon tied to her leg. The nightingale was not very happy.

Then one day a parcel arrived from the Emperor of Japan. Inside the parcel was a mechanical bird made of gold and covered all over with diamonds and rubies and sapphires. When you wound up the bird it sang one of the real

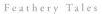

nightingale's songs as its tail went up
and down.

The Emperor clapped his hands
with delight and cried, "Now they can
sing together – a duet!"

And sing together they did. But
somehow it wasn't quite right, for
the wind-up nightingale always sang

exactly the same notes, while the real nightingale sang as she always had, free and flowing and from her heart.

So the wind-up nightingale was made to sing alone. It was just as much of a success as the real nightingale, and it was far prettier to look at because it glittered like jewellery. It sang its song over and over again – thirty-three times in all – and still it wasn't tired.

No one noticed when the real nightingale flew up and away through an open window, back to her own quiet green wood.

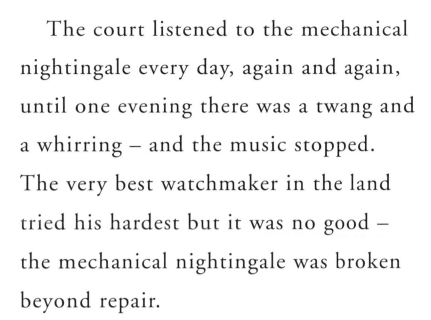

The court listened to the mechanical nightingale every day, again and again, until one evening there was a twang and a whirring – and the music stopped. The very best watchmaker in the land tried his hardest but it was no good – the mechanical nightingale was broken beyond repair.

Time passed and the Emperor fell ill. He lay in his magnificent bed, cold and pale, and everyone at court feared he would die.

In the darkest hour of the night, when Death himself stood in the shadows, the Emperor called out, "Music! I long to hear some music!" But nobody heard him.

Then, quite suddenly, from a branch outside his open window came a familiar sound. The little nightingale was perched there in the moonlight, singing her beautiful song so sweetly that even Death sat up and listened.

"If I sing all night will you let my Emperor live?" asked the little nightingale.

"I will," smiled Death. "But you are only a small bird. You will be exhausted before dawn."

"Not I!" replied the nightingale. She puffed up her feathered chest and sang. She sang of sun on water, of plum blossom and rainstorms and summer breezes. She sang of leaf fall and moonlight in the treetops, until dawn crept over the horizon and Death, defeated, slipped quietly away.

As morning lit the Emperor's bedroom he opened his eyes and looked at the nightingale, still singing.

"Most blessed of little birds," he whispered, "I saw Death at my side last night, but you have sent him away.

How can I ever thank you?"

"You have rewarded me already," said the nightingale. "The very first time I sang for you I brought tears to your eyes. That is all the reward I ever needed."

"Please come back and live with me in the palace again," begged the Emperor. "You shall want for nothing. I will destroy the mechanical bird for it is of no use to me."

"Please, don't do that," said the nightingale, "it did the best it could. And I cannot nest in the palace – I need to fly far and wide and sing for

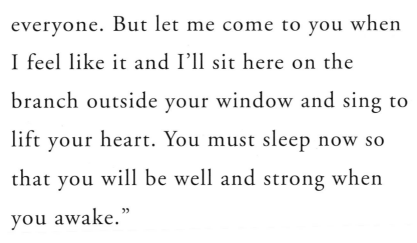
everyone. But let me come to you when I feel like it and I'll sit here on the branch outside your window and sing to lift your heart. You must sleep now so that you will be well and strong when you awake."

The Emperor fell into a deep and refreshing slumber. The sun was shining in on him when he woke and his servants, who had all feared he would be dead by now, stood around his bed and rejoiced!

The Emperor sat up, stretched out his arms in the fresh morning air and said, "Good morning!"

THE JACKDAW
OF RHEIMS

This story is taken from a poem based in Medieval France. The wild spirit of the little jackdaw, who Cardinal Archbishop so loves, cannot be tamed. He is an innocent creature who follows his own instinct and cannot live his life according to our rules.

In all of France there was no court as grand or as splendid as that of the Cardinal Archbishop of Rheims. Even the King's palace in Paris faded into insignificance when compared with that of the Archbishop. Everyone who lived in or near Rheims was curious to see what it was like inside.

When a rumour began to circulate that the Cardinal Archbishop was to hold a great feast to celebrate Christmas, everyone hoped to be invited.

On the evening of the feast, the
guests, dressed in their finest silks and
velvets, crowded into the great hall
of the palace. The tables were lit by
hundreds of flickering candles and piled
high with every delicious thing you
could imagine. There were platters of
roasted meats, stuffed pigeon and swan,
great towers of exotic fruits, honey cakes
and jellies. There were bowls of sweet
oranges, spiced puddings and flagons of
deep ruby wine, and on a spit before the
roaring fire, fine meats were roasting.

The Cardinal Archbishop seated himself in a carved chair at the top table, then signalled that the assembled company should also sit down. The guests stared in awe at the Cardinal Archbishop in his richly embroidered robes, but were amazed when a glossy little jackdaw flew down and perched on his red hat. The Cardinal Archbishop fed the bird little titbits from his plate and smiled indulgently when it flew off to peck at the great platters of food.

"How extraordinary that someone as grand as the Cardinal Archbishop

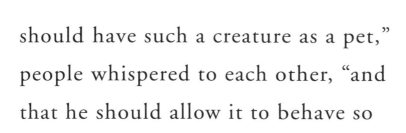

should have such a creature as a pet,"
people whispered to each other, "and
that he should allow it to behave so
badly."

"Disgraceful, if you ask me,"
murmured one guest. "That bird has the
cheek of the devil and dreadfully bad
manners, yet he seems to be the only
creature in the room that the Cardinal
Archbishop really cares for."

But as soon as the food was served,
they all forgot about the jackdaw and
concentrated instead on the delicious
food on their platters and the fine wine
in their goblets. They ate and ate until
they were completely full.

When no one could eat anything

more, six little singing boys dressed
in white came around carrying golden
bowls of water perfumed with lavender
and soft pink towels. The Cardinal
Archbishop carefully took off all his
beautiful rings and laid them to one
side. He was about to wash his hands
when the jackdaw jumped into the
golden bowl, splashing him. The
assembled guests gasped at the creature's
cheek and wondered what the Cardinal
Archbishop would do. But to everyone's
surprise, he just laughed and stroked the
bird's glossy black
feathers.

   The great feast
concluded with

music and entertainments. But just
as everyone was about to leave, the
Cardinal Archbishop let out a huge
shout of anger!

"Stop! No one must leave! Be seated,
every one of you! Someone has stolen
my ring, the one with three diamonds
and two emeralds. It was given to me
by the Pope!"

He turned to his servants. "Search
everyone before they leave. Everyone!
No one is allowed to go until I say so!"

The guests, horrified and
embarrassed, were all thoroughly
searched. Pockets were turned out. Bags,
shoes, gloves and hats were checked.
Every crease and fold of clothing was

searched. But no ring was found.

The Cardinal Archbishop took off his beautiful plum-coloured shoes and looked in the toes. But the ring did not appear.

The monks and the friars and the servants sought high and low, looking in every cupboard and  drawer, behind every curtain, under every carpet and in every nook and cranny. The court was turned inside out and upside down. But the ring was nowhere to be found.

The Cardinal Archbishop was white with rage. "I shall curse this thief as no

one has been cursed before! Whoever
committed this crime will live to regret
it! Bring me my bible!"

Raising one hand and laying the other
on the ancient leather-bound book, the
Cardinal Archbishop intoned:

"In holy anger and pious grief,
I solemnly curse that rascally thief,
I curse him at home
and I curse him in bed,
From the soles of his feet
to the crown of his head,
I curse him in sleeping,
so that every night,
he should dream of the devil
and wake up with a fright.
I curse him in eating,
I curse him in drinking,
I curse him in coughing
and sleeping and winking,
I curse him in sitting,
in standing and lying,
I curse him in walking
and riding and flying,
I curse him in living,
I curse him in dying!"

There was a terrible silence in the great hall. The guests were quaking in their shoes and glancing around to see who was beginning to look unwell.

"Whoever took it will begin to feel poorly in no time," someone whispered.

"I wouldn't be in their boots for anything," agreed his friend.

"No one is looking guilty though," said another.

"Well someone must have done it, and that was the heaviest curse I've ever heard. And from a Cardinal Archbishop too! Someone will begin to waste away before too long, you mark my words."

But no one did. The guests were

eventually sent home, and the monks
and friars and servants continued their
duties. No one showed any sign of
illness, not even so much as a cough or
a headache.

A few days passed. The Cardinal
Archbishop, still in a terrible mood,
asked for his jackdaw. "He hasn't been
here for a while," he said. "It will cheer
me up to see him."

One of the friars climbed up to
the belfry where the jackdaw lived.
But when he reached the nest, he was
shocked by what he saw.
There lay a skinny little bird with
hardly any feathers,
unable to stand, let

alone fly. The jackdaw looked at the friar weakly, made a pathetic little squawk and closed his eyes.

"So you are the thief!" cried the friar. He picked the bird up gently and there,

in among the sticks and straw of the nest, was the Cardinal Archbishop's ring.

The friar ran through the palace calling out to one and all, "It was the Cardinal Archbishop's jackdaw that stole

the ring! Look at him – he's nothing but skin and bone!"

People crowded round and looked at the poor little scrap of black feathers in the friar's hand.

"Well, he got what he deserved," said one.

"Serves him right," said another.

"But that's not fair!" said a little stable boy. "Jackdaws love things that sparkle – they can't help it. He didn't know it was wrong!"

Hearing all the commotion, the Cardinal Archbishop came running.

"What on earth is going on? Did you find my ring? Who is the culprit?"

The friar handed over the ring.

"It was your jackdaw, Your Eminence, Your Holiness. Do you see how effective your curse has been? The bird is at death's door!"

Tears ran down the Cardinal Archbishop's face as he took the scrawny little jackdaw in his hands. He spoke gently: "I absolve this innocent bird of the sin of theft. He was just following his nature and had no sense of it being a crime. Dear God, please lift the curse from my dear friend the jackdaw."

All eyes were on the bird lying in
the Cardinal Archbishop's hands. The
jackdaw opened one beady eye, his claw
twitching slightly, and moved his head
from side to side. The he croaked a
feeble, "Caw".

"Oh, thank the Lord," cried the
Cardinal Archbishop. "My dear jackdaw
is recovering. Bring him some warm
milk and a piece of honey cake. A little
food and a few days' rest and he will be
himself again. The Lord be praised!"

The jackdaw gradually became sleek
and fat again, with a thick crop of shiny
black feathers.

He lived quietly with the Cardinal
Archbishop, but he never went near
anything that shone or sparkled again.
He behaved impeccably for the rest
of his long life, and the bird and the
Cardinal Archbishop were closer
than ever.

THE FIREBIRD

There are many stories of the Firebird, or Phoenix, a mythical creature universally symbolic of immortality. Every hundred years it bursts into flames — and from the ashes, a glorious new bird arises.

I found this story in an old book of Russian fairytales in a second-hand bookshop and loved the descriptions of the prince cradled on the Firebird's back as they soar through the night sky. It feels like a dream ...

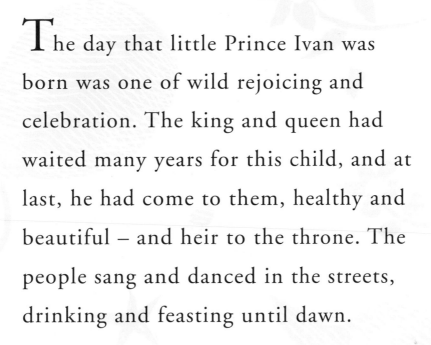

The day that little Prince Ivan was born was one of wild rejoicing and celebration. The king and queen had waited many years for this child, and at last, he had come to them, healthy and beautiful – and heir to the throne. The people sang and danced in the streets, drinking and feasting until dawn.

The next day the king and queen sat gazing at their newborn son when the royal astrologer, a wizened old man called Ferdasan, hurried into the room.

"Welcome, Ferdasan," said the queen. "Come and look at your new prince!"

But the king noticed the look on the old man's face.

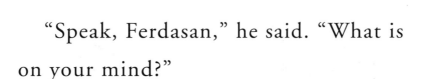

"Speak, Ferdasan," he said. "What is on your mind?"

"I had a dream, Your Majesty, that your son grew fine and healthy, more beautiful and clever with each year that passed…"

The queen smiled. "But of course," she said.

"Please, let me continue, Your Majesty. In my dream, Prince Ivan had reached his fifteenth birthday. On that day, the great Firebird of the Sun swooped down into the palace gardens, just as twilight fell, and the young prince climbed onto his back and they flew away – for ever!"

The queen clutched her baby to her

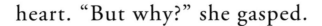

heart. "But why?" she gasped.

"Because your son, Prince Ivan, is destined to marry Aurora, Princess of the Dawn, and this is the only way he can reach her. There is nothing you can do to prevent him going!"

"What do you mean, there's nothing I can do?" roared the king. "I am the king!"

The king and queen kept watch over their son constantly, but as his fifteenth birthday approached they grew more and more anxious. They built a grand tower in the middle of the palace gardens for Ivan and placed guards at the doors. Rich silk and velvet hung at the windows and costly carpets were spread at his feet. All that was missing was company and, of course, freedom.

On the eve of his birthday a wonderful festival began in Ivan's honour. The young prince begged that he might be allowed to at least wander in the gardens on his birthday, but the

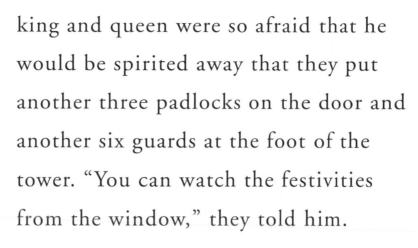

king and queen were so afraid that he would be spirited away that they put another three padlocks on the door and another six guards at the foot of the tower. "You can watch the festivities from the window," they told him.

Ivan watched the celebrations with

mounting frustration. 'I have to leave this place!' he thought. But how was he to escape? He looked at the silken floor-length curtains and had an idea. 'If I tear the curtains into long strips and tie them together, I can make a rope long enough to reach the ground!'

All day long, as sounds of merrymaking drifted up to him in the tower, Ivan tore and knotted and plaited. At last, as evening fell, he was able to quietly lower himself down through the trees and into the garden below.

He wandered along moonlit paths, his heart dancing with delight at being free. As he strayed farther from the castle,

the foliage grew dense and dark and he wondered if he should turn back. But then, in the distance, he saw a misty golden light.

As he got closer, Ivan saw that the source of the light was a great bird with soft feathers of flame, flickering gold and scarlet and lighting up the dark night sky – the Firebird!

Around the Firebird's feathery neck was a portrait of the most beautiful girl Prince Ivan had ever seen.

"This is Aurora, Princess of the Dawn," whispered the Firebird. "Climb on my back and I will take you to her!"

As if in a trance, Ivan climbed up and in a flapping rush of heat and light

the Firebird launched itself into the air.
Soon they were soaring high over the
gardens, then the city, then beyond the
mountains and over the sea. How many
thousands of miles they flew between
the darkest hour and the first light of
morning, the prince could not tell.

He was warm and comfortable,
nestled among soft feathers and lulled to
sleep by the hushing sound of the great

creature's wings as they soared among
the stars.

As dawn broke the Firebird began
to descend, swooping down towards
a beautiful land of hills and streams.

When they finally landed, Ivan stepped onto the grass – and there, waiting to meet him, was the girl in the picture. She was even lovelier than the portrait, and as they looked into each other's eyes, Prince Ivan and Princess Aurora knew that they were meant for each other.

The Firebird spoke: "My work here is done. I wish you all the joy in the world." He plucked a single glowing crimson feather from his chest and placed it gently in Aurora's hair. Then he took off into the sunrise.

There are many kinds of love in this world, but the love that blossomed between the prince and princess was like no other. Aurora felt that she had been dreaming of Ivan all her life, and Ivan felt as if he had arrived in paradise. They wandered, arms entwined, through the meadows and gardens towards the palace where Aurora's parents lived.

But behind a tree, watching from the shadows was Nocturna, Aurora's wicked sister. She had a dark and jealous heart and was skilled in the ways of witches and sorcerers. Instead of feeling pleasure at her sister's happiness, she clenched her hands in a jealous rage.

"I will put an end to this!" she vowed. "Why should they be happy when I am not?" She transported herself to her secret underground chamber and with a

muttering of spells and a stirring of potions she summoned the image of Prince Ivan before her, and with his image came his very soul, so strong was her wicked magic.

Without warning, Ivan clutched at his heart and fell lifeless at Aurora's feet. "No, oh no – Ivan my love!" cried the princess. "Don't leave me so soon! Somebody help me!"

Ivan was carried to the palace and laid on a couch. Aurora held him in her arms, weeping and calling his name as she tried to revive him. His eyes were closed and his lips were pale, but Aurora could sense a faint trembling and she realised that Ivan was not dead – he was merely bewitched.

"Nocturna, this is your doing," she wept. "You have torn his heart from his body, but I know it still beats with love for me! I will find you somehow, I swear!"

But Aurora had no idea where her sister had gone. She ran through the palace and the gardens, searching every dark room and shadowy cave. Despondent, she buried her head in her hands – and felt the glowing feather that the Firebird had placed in her hair.

"Oh, great Firebird, if only you were here!" she wept.

The sky was instantly lit with golden light and there he was – the Firebird in all his glory!

"Jump on my back," he said. "There
is not a minute to lose!"

They flew so fast that they overtook
the setting sun sinking on the horizon.
They headed towards the land of night

and silence, which lies beyond the round
shoulder of the world. The Firebird
blazed along, leaving a trail of light in
his wake, until they came to the Forest-
Without-an-End. The Firebird swooped
down to the mouth of a great dark cave.
As Princess Aurora climbed down from
his back he plucked two more glowing
feathers from his wings.

"Take these feathers to light your
way," he said. "Be warned – you will
need them, for you are about to enter a
very dark place."

Shaking with fear, Princess Aurora
crept into the dripping cave, holding
the radiant feathers high. She had not
gone very far when she heard a voice

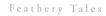

crooning a witchy song. Peering over a
rock, she saw her wicked sister. She was
crouched over a bubbling cauldron on
a freezing fire of ice blue flame that she

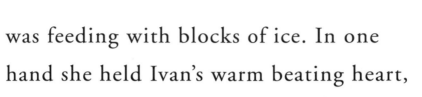

was feeding with blocks of ice. In one hand she held Ivan's warm beating heart, and she sang:

"Into the icy cauldron,

I drop her lover's heart!

I'll hold at bay the light of dawn,

And keep eternal dark!

Never shall their hearts entwine!

Never shall they have joy!

Forever and ever kept apart,

This young girl and this boy!"

With a shriek, Aurora rushed forward and kicked over the cauldron. The freezing liquid in the cauldron spilled over her wicked sister and with a terrible scream, she fell to the floor, frozen forever by her own evil potion.

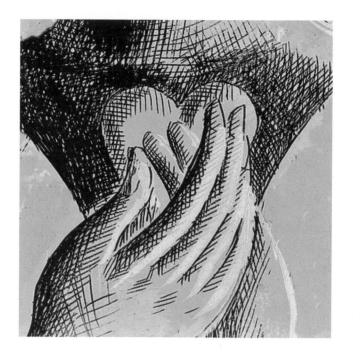

Aurora snatched up her lover's still-beating heart and placed it next to her own. She ran to the Firebird and clambered onto his back once again.

"Back to the palace, dear Firebird, as fast as you can!" she cried. The Firebird flew like a shooting star to where Ivan's lifeless body lay.

Aurora knelt at his side. "Here, my love, here is your heart. I have brought it back to you! All will be well."

Ivan awoke and they clasped each other with delight.

"My sweetest Aurora," said Ivan, "how soon can we be married? It is our destiny to be together."

Aurora's parents were delighted by the match and great celebrations were planned.

Ivan spoke to the Firebird, who was resting in the garden. "Dear Firebird, you are the one who brought us together. How can we ever thank you for such happiness? Do you want gold, or a castle, or forests of your own? Name your wish!"

But the Firebird bent his beautiful glowing head to the prince and said, "All I wish is to bring your poor grieving parents here to you, for they are so unhappy without you. They love you dearly and will be overjoyed to meet your beautiful princess and be a part of your happiness."

So Ivan's parents came to the splendid wedding and were reunited

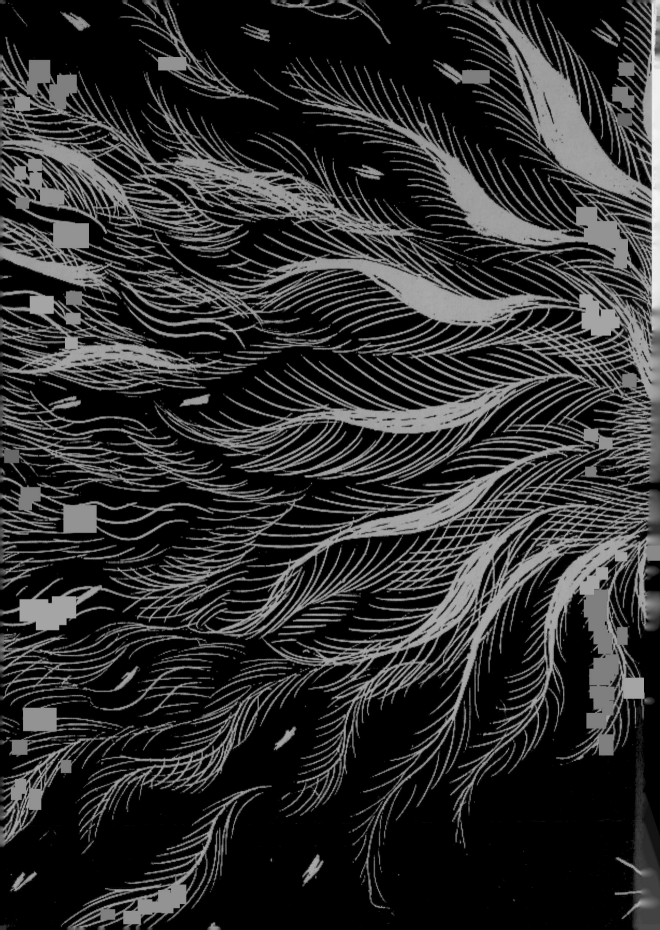

with their beloved son. They came to
love Aurora too, like a daughter. Prince
Ivan and Princess Aurora eventually
ruled the two lands fairly and wisely and
were much loved by their people.

And what of the glowing, kindly
and wise Firebird? He was never seen
again – but on the anniversary of Ivan
and Aurora's wedding day, a single
feather of scarlet and gold was dropped
onto the balcony of their bedroom so
that they could wish for whatever
they needed.

MAGPIE SONG

One for sorrow,

Two for joy;

Three for a girl,

Four for a boy;

Five for silver,

Six for gold;
Seven for a secret
never to be told.
Eight for a wish,
Nine for a kiss,
Ten for a bird you
must not miss.

Acknowledgements and sources

Story research by Ann Jungman and Jane Ray.

The Happy Prince – adapted from the story by Oscar Wilde, Dublin, Ireland (1854–1900).

Mulungu Paints the Birds – from a retelling by Rosalind Whitman adapted from a story told by the Nyamwezi people of Tanzania.

The Owl and the Pussycat – Edward Lear, England (1812–1888).

Noah's Ark – Book of Genesis, Old Testament, The Bible.

Hope is the Thing with Feathers – Emily Dickinson, USA (1830–1886).

The Golden Swan – traditional Indian story, from the Jataka tales, an important part of Buddhist literature, 300 BC.

Jorinda and Joringel – adapted from the Brothers Grimm, German (19th century).

Heron and Hummingbird – a Native American tale from the Hitchiti people, Georgia. This version is taken from two different retellings by Phyllis Doyle and Jenny Williams.

The Emperor's Nightingale – adapted from the story by Hans Christian Andersen, Denmark, (1805–1875).

The Jackdaw of Rheims – a story set in medieval France, from a retelling by Ann Jungman based on the poem by Richard Harris Barham, England (1788–1845).

The Firebird – traditional Russian tale, retold from the version in the Edmund Dulac Fairy Book, France (1852–1953).

Magpie Song – traditional children's nursery rhyme. First recorded in England around 1780.